CHILDREN'S

Oniroku and the Carpenter

retold by
TADASHI MATSUI

Prentice-Hall, Inc., Englewood Cliffs, N. J.

illustrated by
SUEKICHI AKABA

translated from the Japanese by
Masako Matsuno

Oniroku and the Carpenter, (retold by) Tadashi Matsui;
translated from the Japanese by Masako Matsuno

© 1963 by Prentice-Hall, Inc., Englewood Cliffs, N. J.

Library of Congress Catalog Card Number: 63-18116

Printed in Japan

63717-J (T)   63718-J (L)

Once upon a time, there was a wide river
that ran beside a village in Japan.
Its current was so swift
that none of the bridges
built across it ever lasted long.

The people of the village were very unhappy.
Without a bridge, they could not cross the swift river
to go to the market, or to visit their friends.

One day, they all decided to ask a famous carpenter,
who lived in another village,
to build a new bridge.
This carpenter was known as the best bridge-builder
for miles around.

A messenger was sent to the carpenter, who
agreed to take the job when he heard
the village people would pay him
A BIG SUM OF MONEY.

The carpenter went out to look at the river.
Its current was violent.
Can I really build a bridge that will not be
torn apart by the current? he wondered uneasily.

Just then,
many bubbles rose to the surface.
There was a great splashing sound
and the head of an enormous ogre popped
out of the water.

"Hey, man! What's your trouble?" the ogre shouted
in a loud, gruff voice.
"I'm asked to build a bridge over this river,"
answered the carpenter politely.
"Ha!" the ogre shouted with a mean ogre's grin,
"No matter how skilled
you may be,
you cannot build a bridge over this river.
I WON'T LET YOU!"

The carpenter, who could think of no answer,
turned on his heels and started home.
But the ogre bellowed, "Come back, carpenter."
The carpenter stood facing the ogre again.

"I will build your bridge," said the ogre.

"I will pay you most of my BIG SUM OF MONEY
if you do," said the carpenter.

"I do not want your money," said the ogre.
"I only want something that you will not need
after the bridge is built."

"What is that?" asked the carpenter in a scared voice.
(He knew that ogres like to make mean bargains.)

"YOUR EYES!" shouted the ogre in glee.

The poor carpenter fled in terror.

The next day the carpenter went to the river again.
He had made up his mind to find a way
to build that bridge himself. He did not want
to give his eyes to the ogre.

But when he got to the river, he saw
a beautiful, strong bridge already half-built.

On the following day, the bridge was completed.
It was the strongest, most handsome bridge
the carpenter had ever seen.

Just then, the terrible ogre appeared.
"I have built your bridge," he shouted.
"Now you must give me your eyes!"

"But I did not PROMISE to give you my eyes,"
said the poor carpenter in a small, scared voice.
"Is there nothing I can give you instead?"

The ogre grunted and growled.
But finally he said,
"Within a week you must either guess my name
or I will come and get your eyes."

The carpenter fled without a word.

The carpenter ran up one side of a mountain
and down the other side. He sloshed through
rice paddies and fields of grain.
At nightfall he came to an enchanted wood.

Suddenly, a strange voice sang:
"Eyes, eyes, the carpenter's eyes—
Pray come to me soon with ONIROKU—
I'm waiting, waiting, waiting for you . . ."
And the strange singing stopped.

"Hulla!
ONIROKU must be the ogre's name,"
said the carpenter to himself
as he started home feeling peaceful and glad.
He slept soundly that night
for the first time since he had met the ogre.

The next morning, the carpenter went to the river
to have a little fun with the ogre.

"Give me your eyes," shouted the ogre,
sputtering water.

"Give me the chance to guess
your name, instead," pleaded the carpenter.

"All right," said the ogre.
"But of course you won't succeed.
No one can ever guess an OGRE'S name."

"Your name is Gawataro," shouted the carpenter.
"I would NEVER have a name like THAT," said the ogre.

"It's Gongoro," shouted the carpenter
who was really beginning to enjoy himself.

"No such thing!" said the wicked ogre,
grinning from ear to ear.

The carpenter pretended to be quite desperate.
"Could it be Daitaro?" he asked timidly.

"Wrong! Wrong! Wrong!"
bellowed the ogre.
"Hand over your eyes!"

The carpenter now knew it was time
to tell the ogre his name.

"Your name is . . .

O - NI - RO - KU!"

the carpenter shouted in a loud voice.

The grin left the ogre's face—
without a word he vanished.

In a minute, there was nothing to be seen
but the swift-running river
and the handsome, strong bridge.